Giving Thanks

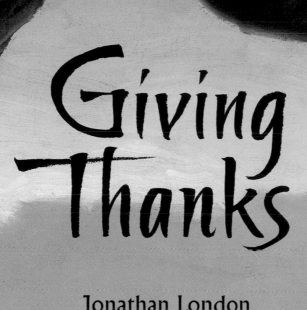

Giving Thanks

Jonathan London

paintings by Gregory Manchess

CANDLEWICK PRESS

"Thank you, Mother Earth.
Thank you, Father Sky.
Thank you for this day."
This is what my father says,
every morning,
standing in the field
near our house.

Like his Indian friends—
singers and storytellers—
Dad believes that the things of nature
are a gift. And that in return,
we must give something back.
We must give thanks.

He gives thanks
to the frogs and the crickets
singing down by the creek—
and to all the tiny beings
with six or eight legs,
weaving their tiny stories
close to the earth.

He says "Thank you"
to chanterelles,
the wild mushrooms that smell
like pumpkins.

He says "Thank you"
to the trees
that wave their arms
and spin their leaves
in the breeze.

He says, "Thank you,
Fox," at a glimpse
in the tall grass—
the pointy ears,
the bushy tail
dancing.

He says "Thank you"
to the deer
who have passed this way,
their tracks like two fingers
pressed in the dirt,
pointing toward water.

He gives thanks
to the quail
who flare up and scatter
and rejoin.

He says, "Thank you,
Jackrabbit," as it zigs
and zags and jumps in leaps
twenty-five feet
through the air,
racing a shadow.

He says, "Thank you,
Hawk," as it circles
high in the sky
and cries *scree! scree!*
before it dives.

He says, "Thank you,
Grandfather Sun,"
as it begins to sink
beyond the hills.
"Thank you for this day."

And he says, "Thank you,
Grandmother Moon,
for coming this way."

To me, it's a little
embarrassing
to say thanks
to trees and things.
But Dad says it becomes a habit;
it makes you feel good.

"Thank you, stars," I say
as we near home.

And the stars come out,
one by one,
as if from hiding.

For Joe Bruchac, again,
and for Lanny Pinola and Julian Lang, with thanks
J. L.

For my father,
whose silent prayers inspired my curiosity about the world
G. M.

Text copyright © 2003 by Jonathan London
Paintings copyright © 2003 by Gregory Manchess
Calligraphy by Judythe Sieck

First paperback edition in this format 2011

The Library of Congress has cataloged the hardcover edition as follows:

London, Jonathan, date.
Giving thanks / Jonathan London ; paintings by Gregory Manchess. — 1st ed.
p. cm.
Summary: A father teaches his son to celebrate
the interconnectedness of the natural world through daily words of thanks.
ISBN 978-0-7636-1680-9 (hardcover)
[1. Prayer—Fiction. 2. Nature—Fiction. 3. Fathers and sons—Fiction.
4. Indians of North America—Fiction.] I. Manchess, Gregory, ill. II. Title.
PZ7.L8278 Gi 2003
[Fic]—dc21   2002023750

ISBN 978-0-7636-2753-9 (first paperback)
ISBN 978-0-7636-5594-5 (reformatted paperback)

11 12 13 14 15 16 CCP 10 9 8 7 6 5 4 3 2 1
Printed in Shenzhen, Guangdong, China

This book was typeset in Flareserif.
The paintings were done in oil on linen.

Candlewick Press
99 Dover Street
Somerville, Massachusetts 02144

visit us at www.candlewick.com